What Weaponry

What Weaponry

Elizabeth J. Colen

a novel in
prose poems

Black
Lawrence
Press

Black
Lawrence
Press

www.blacklawrence.com

Executive Editor: Diane Goettel
Book and Cover Design: Amy Freels
Cover Art: "Vacation, 2013", oil on board, Justin Duffus

Copyright © Elizabeth Colen 2016
ISBN: 978-1-62557-957-7

Published 2016 by Black Lawrence Press.
Printed in the United States.

The heart's a mouth, and fuck its reasons.
—Rachel Loden

(CONTENTS)

(1)

LOW CLOUDS

We build a place to be safe, start talking in circles and so build that way. We start with small stones, then large. We work quietly. Our concentric circles grow. Wet sand cold under our toes. We move on to driftwood, again starting small: with what we might use for fire if we stay too long. Then the big ones: white logs as big as we can haul them. Fourteen circles in all, crabs lumber over them, dry kelp blows at one edge. The dog is careful, having been told. She goes back into the ocean, which is ruining the last, widest circle into a C. We lay in what we have made, minute fleshy bullets in the target we have made.

When we see it from above we will know the sea is near, as is the grey, as is the end. When we see it from above the plane will be circling, destroying low clouds. When we see it from above we will be listening, we will be watching, we will go there as fast as we can.

WAITING FOR THE DAMAGE

I will say everything I can say and then you will say
something too. There is anger in both of us, fusing
the closer we get. For now we stand at the lip of the
world, waves lapping grey stones under a grey sky:
our little world. There is **something** to this.
Something that wants to be calm, to be easy. "Look
at that," you say, pointing out far in the ocean. I nod,
but see nothing. I'm willing to look anyway.

The dog brings a stick. There is bravery to the womb
of her **mouth** keeping wood in, **seawater** out as she
huffs the stick back in from where we toss it: out
there.

BREADFRUIT

You choose any moment rather than this one. Listen to the cat **hemmed** in by dogs who won't do anything. "They tease," you say and still stare out at the **sound**. It's a few blocks over and still you stare. "You know that painting?" you say. "What one?" "Cezanne's Paysage." I have no idea what you're saying and so shrug like I don't care you've made another reference I can't latch to. "I want trees," you say. But we both know how we go to fresh air like fish, gasping. And the time we tried to make love in the back of the truck, which had filled partly with dropped plums, overripe and messy. Juice stained **our skin and our clothes**. We looked butchered. And then there were the ants. "You don't want that," I say. And you say, "Sure I do," which is also what you said about living together and look how that's gone. "I think she got away," you say, face to pane, but then the mewling starts up again.

FANCY THAT

For this she thanks God, your sister, little wonder. Little mercy, ten fingers, ten toes. In sin we learn to count again. How many messes made at another's expense. "How much does an abortion cost?" you asked back then. But she's new now. And how many? Like, *a girl never tells her age.* She might have said Fuck You, but you told her it's something you'd never know. Not without a phone call. Baby's on hold; it's called sleeping. "And what did you name him?" "Her." Then the baby cries. "What did you name her?" *Fancy.* All the love you'll ever need.

CARTOGRAPHY

You are six years old. Your brother is blind. Your brother is blind with his hands over his eyes. Your brother is not really blind. The divorce has done this to him. Dust and sadness has done this to him. Motion sickness has done this to him. And the sun in his eyes. He wants to be blind. He wants to be you. In the front seat: you. Hands in your lap. You make a strangling motion, twisting your pants at the knees. Your mother in the driver's seat beside you doesn't know the pant legs are her, the bunched-up fabric her throat. Brother strops his hand in his lap every time a locust exoskeleton breaks on the windshield, irregular beats, but often. It is *that* year. You are escaping. You are escaping joy and the reaching fingers of the boy next door. You are escaping your father locked out of the house, his palm drumming your bedroom window. To be let in is to give in. **It means** you've done wrong. Open the map. Let the paper cut your palm. Mother blinks **too often**. Put your hand on the dashboard, redsmear. This is where we're going. Put your hand on her wrist. Put your hand on the wheel.

YOUR MOTHER KNOW YOU RIDE LIKE THAT

She bought the cheapest bicycle. Light pink around its middle. You were standing in the road to be **standing in the road**. You shut the color off and focused on the freedom. When grandpa died you were mad they wouldn't open his eyes for you. You said you could ride and pushed to the end of the drive. You were six years old. You'd never seen a corpse before. You'd never held a bike. Legs still bruised from riding handlebars. You pumped the pedals harder. Your mother pinched your hand until you left the coffin. You cried, never to see his eyes again. "The blue," you said, "just one more time." The neighbors shook their heads. You flew then, legs above your braces. When you came to a man was standing over, harsh sunlight piercing from behind his neck and shoulder. And then you took his hand.

A DROWNING, 1984

A woman with wet hair walks by. You want her to be
your mother. And so you follow her. Her green and
white sandals go **click-click** and it's like the
heartbeat **you can't remember**. You want to be on
that boat in the wind, head to her chest. **Click-click**
on the gum-covered pavement. In your head those
fifteen, eighteen, twenty-two steps behind her you
change her hair brown to red. **You change** her
lipstick, which is easy from the back. You only saw
her mouth for a moment. It did not make a kissy face
into the glass as she passed. A woman's mouth can
do anything. Click-click. Though the street is full of
motion, she looks at no one. She does not turn her
head. A car backfire, some siren. A loud shout from
a boy to a man on the street's other side. Even this
does not make her turn. For all you know she could
be deaf, water logging her ears. You call out *mother*,
but she doesn't respond. You call out *monster,* but
she keeps moving ahead.

WHAT FANCY SAID

I bury one knee-deep in red dirt. Limber, waist-bent, the dilly-doll—what your niece called it—bows or leans its head upon a mound. Fancy chuckles, pulls it out, wrecks its hair with weeds, disassembles clothing. Fancy wears the same red shoes. Fancy gets a bee sting. She hums and waters, floods delphinium, phlox, nasturtium with a broken bucket until torn plastic tears her hand. Your sister buttons up baby, stumbly on stubby legs, fleshy knees wet with mud, arms stuck with blood. Your sister swabs baby blood while we continue playing, muscling roots up to tickle Fancy's wrapped palm. Little **disaster** in pink frills. **Little** disaster reminds me. Little angel, **monster**, mystery. She never cries. Your sister's shouts echo backwards into the trees. Nothing bad has ever happened to her. Nothing ever will. Your sister shouts at your bad language. Says, "Look how pa ended up." "Frickin," **you** say. "Frickin," Fancy says.

THE URN

On a trip to the beach you store ashes under your passenger seat: mother and father mixed together in one raw torrent of dust. **Made of bone**, stone urn encases. We wrap rubber bands around it, base to top. There is no latch and it rolls. After every abrupt stop you lean back to check. "Mom and pop," you call them. You never called them this. Your sister will meet us. She will be crying already when we get there, saying, "I can't look at this, I can't look at this" when you unearth what's left of them. She will lean against a grey pier, her face more grey, the baby wanting more of her, sand, more of her, salt and hair and dust in everyone's eyes. You will snake the rubber bands around your wrist once, twice, three times, tighter. You will leave them there all day.

EPISODIC TREMOR AND SLIP

None of us will notice the sunbathers, the tourists trying to surf, the tourists trying to sail. **We won't see** the parade of push-pop wrappers scattered in wet sand, we won't see the cops or the dog **watching**, or the kelp strangling posts of the pier.

THE PUBLIC SHOWERS

A fat man in a tight swimsuit asks a young girl to wash his back. We pretend we don't see this. The sun in our eyes, or grit kicked up by passing bicycles. There's a painting on a cinderblock wall, a Middle Eastern scene, or maybe it's meant to be here to show there's more to the beach than tan and pale blue. More than unwatched ice cream stands and children shattering day with the din clang of laughter or some imagined pain. Two women sit in shadow, lean against a fake checkered floor that rises behind them into smaller and smaller black and white squares. "Depth perception," you say. One woman says to the other woman, "It was just easier to go along." An immaculate palm reaches over everything, dark paint of shade, a coned building dwarfed and chapped by sun. Because this isn't a **real scene**. This isn't what we wanted. Something exotic lives here, but it isn't in the paint or the sand. It's not in the lorikeets resting on tanned arms or shit-covered pylons. Not in the Queen Mary, or the Spruce Goose hangar. Or the gulls rocketing away from the shore. It's not in the restless hum of waves trashing the beach with wet sacks of potato chips and broken glass. It's not in you or in me, but then we find it.

MEMORY OF LIGHT

A star is a memory of light. What we can't see from here. What is talked about. Cities either have wars or no history at all. We were one here, bodies bent back against concrete, pressed into wood, pressed into glass, last looks at the loved. Standing on Pike or Pine, we smell the salt of the ocean, but it's only the sound, broken off from the real water by mountains, forests of rain, tumult of wildness before wild. Ferries drift like **satellites across black water**. You've forgotten why **we**'ve come and I don't answer; it's best to come to this knowledge alone. In the hotel at the top of the hill bricks **bristle** when the ground moves. We stand in a quiet side street, two blocks from the hospital, close to each other and parked cars. I say, "In the 1950s builders on the west coast stopped using bricks." I don't know if this is true, but I like it. Brick ovens bake bricks, clay and mortar grow homes, hotels. "Because of earthquakes?" you ask. I wanted something different, another word. It's *tremblement de terre* in French, **trembling** of earth, *terremoto* in Spanish, like some forward movement, sounds like an automobile. The water **swells** in different names. The ground swells, fault, pipes sweat a mess in the street. A groundswell is something **without land**. I wanted another word, but all I say is "yes," which answers everything. "Tu a peur?" "Yes." "Tu a faim?" "Yes." Oui and oui and oui and oui. The street calms and nothing falls, not bricks or anything. I look up; the skyline is still. Planes go on moving. Even cars haven't noticed a thing. In one hotel window, a man stands bare-chested. He doesn't see us on the street. When he moves back into the room his window becomes one more yellow square.

BUCKSHOT AND DIESEL

My uncle died when his John Deere rolled over him,
muddied cornfield and gravity, my aunt's descent
into madness. She chalked her papered walls with
manure, pocked them with buckshot. I mentioned
this before, but **not** the hollow sound the husks
made when she was gone, like **unreadable** Bible
pages bleached in sun, shushing in wind. In the hall
was a pencil drawing of someone who looked like
Uncle holding the hand of someone small—maybe
me—and when asked she said it's Beelzebub and
pancakes or papyrus. Maybe pansies or papaya—
something with a p. I can't remember anymore.
They say to call up memory think of something
quotidian, so I think of the morning's obituaries
(only old dead), sports scores, patterns of mown
grass, and the press of penises inside sweatpants at
the gym. None of which bring anything back **but** the
vague discomfort I started with. When auntie said
Beelzebub I slapped her, though it wasn't my place.
My miscalculation enfolds now on linens made of
silk, or some high thread count. The sheets shine so
we can almost see ourselves, *like* ourselves. You lean
back, our eyes close, it's nothing like the house fire,
nothing like the diesel stench puddled in the field.

CONTAMINATION ANXIETY, NO. 1

I love *you* **when**—you told me not to talk that way. We went down to the 76 to buy some cigarettes; Ralph's was cheaper, Camels on sale, but the road was so wide, four lanes, five lanes, six at the light. There was a man at the station flicking lit matches at the pumps, not getting far, but far enough to make me nervous. Far enough that **I put my palm on the big red button**, the emergency stop the whole time you were inside, grappling over a nickel with the handsome, turbaned man. I'd told him the day before I liked his moustache—and it's true—I have a thing for them. But he thought I was joking. "I'm never joking," I said. And I forgot to get my change.

CONTAMINATION ANXIETY, NO. 2

We should have **known** that eventually the boy would become more interesting. *I like the way you swim*, he said. And we were at superlatives quickly. *You're the best diver; you've got the nicest feet; calves; shins.* I wanted his leg like a cigarette hanging off my lip; I wanted to bite him. We should have known that eventually we would draw names. **X** was at the top of the list, **X** was second. I wanted both, but lines were drawn.

CONTAMINATION ANXIETY, NO. 3

There **we** were in the hotel **hot** tub across the street. I mean, not supposed to be, but there. Dented beer cans and a joint swollen by splash. I was in love and I let him. I wasn't in love. He was high and did what he wanted, until some couple wandered in. I was stupid. I mean, I was in love with him. It's still not right when I say it. Having nothing, I'd give it all. My breath held like in mother's car with the windows rolled up and the chain-smoking and the boyfriend who punched her in the side of her head. **When** I was a child I was a forest on fire. But there I was in the tub trying to separate two years of ruin and what my body did when I thought of the boy. I sang "Jessie's Girl" in my head. But replaced the Jessie with **X. Yes**. "Kiss my neck," I said, thinking that part less discerning. But he was still hard, still smelled like the wrong kind of boy.

NOT A PLEASANT LOVER

I had a dream I was not a pleasant lover and you were not a pleasant lover and **we spread it around**. Sheets of fire covered sheets of plain, grass bled black soot that cooled. I apologized, begged you like a liar. The wound over my eye took three weeks to heal. No one asked about it. No one wants to know. In your throat, choked sigh. Sleep stays gummed. And you were never sorry. Sorry, you were never used. Music adjacent to music in another fallow room, another chair fallen over. Thunder, chord, clouds darken like the last page turning. Weather turning like the yellow star of bruise.

SHOT-SILK EFFECT, NO. 1

In the morning we wake to sharp sunlight through
the lone pine or hemlock outside our motel window.
"What *is* that?" you say. "I don't know what *kind* it is,
if that's what you're asking." We can't come to any
conclusion. The trees are tall here, ambitious. They
are like the kids in high school no one can touch.
Through the tree we can see more trees, and deep
blue shapes of sky through them. When you lean
way out, a corner of the parking lot becomes clear,
grey asphalt glistens silver and **your face lights up.**

SHOT-SILK EFFECT, NO. 2

The newspaper stains your hands and you keep reaching up to push your hair out of your eye. Fat strand greasy and it won't stay put. A black mark runs across your brow. Headlines scream, but I can't read them; the light is too bright. I just listen to the paper being moved by your hands, the slick ads sliding to a mess on the floor. I was a page-turner in high school for the man who ran the orchestra. He used to navigate my thighs with the tip of his baton. I suddenly think about where he is now, what he's doing, if he's dead yet. I think about his wife's dyed yellow hair. But instead I say, "I wonder what was destroyed. If anyone was killed." In the earthquake I mean, but I don't say it. Something rumbles the next street over and you look up at a nothing space on the wall and I know we both think: *aftershock* while we wait for the plaster to crack and crumble. But then there's the *beep-beep* of the truck backing up.

SHOT-SILK EFFECT, NO. 3

You want to shower, but the water's brown no matter how long you run it. You sit back down. There's a plane crash on TV, but it's someplace we've never heard of. "Not many, I'm sure. If any at all. Probably none." And it takes me a minute to remember what we've talked about. *The dead.* It's always the dead. I don't know why any of this should make you smile, but **your face breaks open** like a crowd at a sporting event.

SHOT-SILK EFFECT, NO. 4

We read the paper. Or I sit and watch as **you do**. We turn the TV volume down so low we can't hear anything but mumbling that could be the people in the room next door. When I look up, I see beached whales pixelated, a bad image and stretched fat the way things look on flat-screen TVs. I wonder if the whales have to do with the earthquake or if it's simply the oil again. You tear into another orange and the room smells nice and the wet runs quick down your arm. "I had a dream last night—" I start, but then decide I don't want to tell you.

OTHERWISE, EMPTY

I had a dream last night the girl had me tied to a bed.
Not **our** bed, but something like it, dark wood and
haunted with all the things we'd done. Bars like
prison, bars to be tied to. But thick and iron like the
threaded pipe we found next to your father's head.
When this is over, I'm sure to have more nightmares,
but for now it's only hollowed trees, infinite walls of
water. And then this dream last night; she had me
bound. And I don't remember much, just her face in
profile, hands in the mirror, fingers up and counting
or pointing. Directing the action in her little show.
Someone was playing mah-jongg in the next room.
Through the open door I could see smoke and hear
the telltale clacking of tiles. Then the cackling of
women who have such stillness in them that their
throats simply open up without their consent.
Someone said, "Rack of lamb." And I thought, *Lamb
of God?* Then she shut the door. The room seemed to
spin. "Balanced," she said. I wished I could touch
her. "On the head of a pin."

(2)

SOMEONE WITH KEYS

We wait for someone with keys. The dry grass, ankle-deep, is pocked brown with rotting apples. "An orchard," you say to me or to the two trees. A bee examines one sweet corpse, feet settling in sickly syrup. Across the street a mower chokes out, starts up again. The man handling it could be thirty, could be sixty, could be your father **back from the dead**. Mower hits a rock and the blades scream. The man looks which way the rock went and mows down iris. Eye god in the nursed dirt, purple explodes in the bed. The wife looks from the window, glances over at us, pulls the curtain. "Friendly," I smile, but you don't notice. I look at your hands, which are soft and nothing like his. You fidget again, pulling a leaf off the tree. You frayed the map the whole way here, determined turns while I took my time at the wheel. "Can you go faster?" I pushed my heel in for the speed up, but knew we'd be early. Like most things, this was your call. I turned the radio loud. Bob Dylan, like an angel of mercy came on, singing something we both knew. Now your hands fondle the gate latch, fold tree leaves into squares, then back to the latch. "I like what your voice does when you don't know the words," I say. But you probably don't hear me. Your face follows a truck as it turns up the street, approaches, then sails past. The first night we stay here we will push what's left of your father's things into the back yard, we will watch bats circle the trees.

THE PERFECT KIND OF HAPPY

From one window I can see the water and from the other I can see the mountains. These are not real mountains, this is not real water, these are not real windows. I hold your hand or I strike **you** or you strike me or **light up a cigarette** and our upstairs disappears. But what if we're in it? I think of particles exploding, coming back together like some physics experiment I don't know the name for. "Large Hadron Collider," you say.

But that's not what I mean.

*

For a long time when you were a child you thought you didn't exist if **your** mother wasn't with you. What was *this* called? You were invisible and no one spoke to you and the silence supported the **theory**, except for the bells ringing in doorways and the tap of your loose shoelace. "But did you pass through walls?" I ask and you say this has nothing to do with *perte de vue*. You lay under chairs while weight creaked the springs. Your mother's hand came into the frame and you were real again, visible, whole.

ORDERS OF MAGNITUDE

"Child abuse is a metaphor," you say. Your father never hit you. But then this, too, is no longer true. It was the neighborhood kids who put pieces of themselves into your hair, it was them who made you bleed. Bullets of blood on your forehead, how the scalp will leech into a collar, red circle **of** love around your neck.

ON SNOW

It's an active volcano, the mountain, Shuksan. We live in an earthquake zone, calm north on the Ring of Fire. The house is on stilts for the waves, and rats eat tea biscuits and leave on suggestion. "We will live forever," you say, meaning them. And the water looks brilliant from here. Silver, pellucid, much like the **sky**.

DUPLICATION

Some mornings stab the breath right out of our **lungs**. A rooster crows, sound lightning through the unkempt clutch of trees. The highway, like water, wanders off when the wind picks up. Your mother used to bake bread that looked like the **dark stones** we find **on the beach**. You fill each pocket, remembering when bread was heavier. That golden bough, that blackened char that made the mouth right, made the mouth into a Turing machine. This is what success is: talking to each other with our fists up, a rotating cuff. Guilt is a function of Consequence, equals Risk times Possibility. A stab is a throb is a heartbeat. We make love that sinks in shallow water, love that floats the deep. The camera is another face in the crowd, the room an engram. A way to get right with oh my God.

EXPANDED CINEMA

This morning before the dog walk I put an extra layer on. I kept thinking about the body in the cold water, the sky so morning cold. There'd been rumors all week. But there were no wounds and nothing was bruised. Pink shirt held under water? How easy death comes.

I used to dream of bullet wounds. In thighs, just a maim. They say to dream of **red legs** is to live through lust. They say life is full of holes. That all matter, if condensed, could fit into a sphere the size of a pea. I say bullet. Yes—let's get this to go.

RAVINE

"Let's have a conversation everyone in the world has had." You're standing **in the creek bed**, hand against your eye. The sun is low, atonal, as the day goes. "If this was your last day what would you do?" "But the day is almost over," I say. "And you've wasted it?" When you move your feet, the wet climbs higher on your leg and there's the sound of stones—like they're deep inside a cavern or from some other time. Light takes eight minutes from the sun or moon. Water circles your ankle in a tear shape. You've become just another obstacle. I smell the raw husk of sex or that spot behind your neck, the sweat. Light pulls through trees like so many bits of metal, between the scratched glass and the blood, buzz and concrete. We've been gone all day. I want to tell you how a swallow finds his home by the sun or plate tectonics. "No one's ever asked me that," I say. Strange compass of feather **and** hollow bone. "So?" I have no ready answer. If the day ends, if I end with **the** day, I don't know whether you mean this is my last or *our* last. I can't see the planet existing without me. If it's the end of me, I'll lie down and look at the sky, but if the sky's gone—   Crows stalk parallel branches, mathematical, **precise**. Fisted rock is a **function of awe** and potential. Someday soon I'll have nothing to lose.

A MORE SUPPLE PERPLEX

You're beneath the veil again, newspaper hatchery, wild with thoughts. We haven't gotten the mail in eight days and **you want to say it's** conspiracy. The neighbors don't like us, let's leave it at that. The coffee pot sputters and you jump. **It's** not a growl, **it's** machinery. I pour a little brandy in your cup when you get up to check the stove: row of **dazzling** nozzles, row of buttons, fear the flare of fire, if absent, the gas. You turn towards the door, touch the key rack twice. "Gasoline," you say. "I must go into town." I nod and you nod, knowing I won't go. I can see you at the post office counter again, and the man behind it with his impeccably pressed shirt, just as I'm watching you. "This town doesn't want us," you'd say again if I went with you. One the way back, we'd be careful with our lines. We would stop for ice cream or cigarettes or both because I wanted something to do with my hands.

DIAGRAM OF A CAMERA

Red dirt highlights Fancy's red hair. I take every quarter from the jar. Turn it over. You've brought her here to show her where the last snowfall dented the eaves. "We weren't even here when it snowed." And then the sword she won't stop talking about, frown of scabbard in the hall. Your father's trophy from another lost war. We forgot the broken camera at the pawnshop, pieces of us jammed inside like a punched-in wall that dimples but won't fail. The ticket was light, **a feather in blue**, blue pen. The dog stands perfectly still. You start slicing apples and figs and then slip, start with a clock and end with a copy of *Shōgun*, a rough julienne. Fancy cries, holds her thumb, looks to the foyer, as if willing some authority figure there. "We don't talk about doors," you say. It's too much like leaving, too much like running away. When the sobs fade into gentle interruptions, you push a gumball into her small hand, holding it there so long your fingers sweat together in a mess of unnatural blue.

NO SMOKING, NO OPEN FLAMES

Severed and scabbed birdwing, integer in the wild cream froth of road. Earthwork the men had forgotten, one of those blinking A-frames, orange stripes, the gaudy luster of diastole, narrowing. The torn stalks of some messy bouquet. There is sinister in the shut down, in the gravel in the road, of knowing hemlock, dirty socks, and unlocked doors. The pain was accidental, the value of a rub questioned. Smudges the shape of some giant thumb. This was my sympathy, too. Rain runnels in the runoff grate, gurgle in the birdsong, moan in the mention. Say **you** didn't **s**ay **h**is name. Say you **s**a**ng it**.

THROATLATCH AND LONGEING

Across the trees we hear hooves beating, dark thud of bone on grass, bone on hard mud. Or a fist buried in a heavy bag. Thawed chicken hitting the floor, what's more of a splat. Flat shoes on fresh concrete. What might fall down stairs, into dirt cellars. What your mother was once. **Fist buried in** a silent stomach. Muffle of rifle, forestock and barrel wrapped in a pillow. You and your brother learned to shoot guns with no one looking, no one to hear. High pitch of a burnt hand. Plastic melts on the stovetop vortex of filament you can't take your eyes from. Sudden wind through narrow woods. High pitch of wet timber cut fast. The tractor's loose timing belt. The neighbor fucking his wife, the neighbor **breaking** his horse.

ARROW IN THE TALL GRASS

Arrow in the tall grass. Fancy stands in memory and daddy's wingtips, who could buy her clothes. **Pink** things think **things through**. Girls divide with shadow, a high pitch, receptacle of violence. Arrows in the dune again trailing wind like thunder, but you were broken glass. Bottle shoved, and you were shrug. Or something was imagined. We took a walk in weeds. Dumb moths powdered our arms, alit on fringed grass of Parnassus. Low sun dodged clouds, made Rorschach out of trees. On the street, some Chevy so low to the ground it didn't have a shadow. I imagined her ball stuck under, then Fancy, legs out, nothing moving. What would be our fault. But the ball didn't go there and Fancy was fine. Then you told that story about dead people on a boat, live people on the shore. There were ropes and hopelessness. Everyone lined up, flexed muscles, said, "We've got to get them in here." The islands were electric with blue, but that was just the sea spray. Someone attached rope to a circle of firs, tough bark for a rubbing. Afternoon made longer by low tide, dirtier. But then you said you made it up, and I was with you. Fancy out of earshot, screaming at the trees. **A story or a lie is** just a truer thing.

THE CODES OF EVENTUAL LOVE

I wake to find the dog dead, frozen to the porch outside. She wasn't our dog, but something like a mascot and even saying *wasn't* instead of *isn't* when she's still there paws to the step, fur matted on the screen door, is to admit there's something unreal about us too. Arm muscle twitching all night, it was like some kind of dance to be next to you in bed. I had to stay on the move to keep from being hit. Like sleep's **some kind of excuse**. Overgrown rose scrapes across the window, a pitch outside of aural, the hair stands on my neck. **I think I** should have known. The codes of eventual love mean we will adore *something* someday. Your mother lived with her parents while pregnant with you. She tore thorns from her hair with no sense of how they got there. Mute rodents followed her nightly through the woods. Mute appendages, she stole digits, tobacco-stained futures, thin-papered, fragrance worn through the nose until her eyes **wa**tered with the brilliance of attention. *Will you look at me?* Your mother **s**tacked baby books at the side of her bed, but they were **the wrong kind** and she never read them: How to Raise Sheep for Wool, How to Tend Goats, The Joy **of** Milking. What made babies want to live? She could feel your desolation the same as your shifting foot. Dark little tool. When you were born your father was stationed some distant elsewhere with more willing women than postcards.

Your grandmother chewed her hair while grandpa held the needlework, forcing the metal tip in the space between his knuckles. You were a colicky **baby**, prone to fits of stentorian wail. You were born with a brown bead closed in your pink fist just below the skin. No one could pry it out without disturbing slumber. So it stayed.

WE ARE ONLY ANIMALS FURRED AND UNDONE

In this land time stops, white bird hovering in the pre-dawn. Unseen fawns high step the wet grass. And we, feet and shins bathed in shallow seas of scrub, marvel at the complete dark. "There's nothing," you whisper, and then say nothing more. I know you mean the world has closed down its doors. We haven't slept but tired's come back to wild elation the way all things circle back to meet their opposites. The way I sometimes become you again. And through bare toes feeling for the towpath, and that stab of electric light moved on by our motion, we find the neighbor's barn door. **No light** in neighbor's kitchen, no horse sounds from the yard. **Only** the crickets and your **breathing**, pale face posed, the gun still in your hand.

RED ANGLES OF A CURIOUS PAST

So much of who you are is in this shadow on the wall. Bullfight hunger and me, **stupid in my best red shirt**. Arms outstretch against the leaden slag of a century's wear, a century's seen blood bath, violent rigor, bent horns' blister and all of that. Of light striping the eaves, a population of swallows flower and retreat and you're with them, listening for the scrape of exit, bone-colored flap of the replacement board. Hear how it whistles high-pitched like the brittle failure of a hundred conversations. See how the brainchamber empties, loses its vault of stars backwards into the hay.

INSIDE THE LOST MUSEUM

This town smells like a campfire this morning. It's burning up, one building at a time. Century-old storefronts explode like Roman candles, white smoke lines townie lungs, water flows uphill from spent hoses, slickening the streets, throwing street lights back at the sky. Lost inside the quaint museum. All totem poles, daguerreotypes of industry men, and quilts from someone's bed. "Maybe they take them back home at night." How to spread even after everyone's seen. How to **still** warm. Coffee circle over one yellow square. **St**ain on grape appliqué, auburn oblong like blood or chocolate or mud from some tiny fist. Tell me more about your father's felled trees. Pine and aspen, sequoia, juniper, hemlock. Skagit River Tug and Schooner Bella. One Log Road and Steam Skimmer, White Logger. Saw one half open-mouthed smile, saw the other half just below. Scream in the woods like some rush to forgiveness. Creak in your arm, pulling splinters.

WEIGHTLESS

Any line I like to question. You draw one on the kitchen floor in powdered sugar and cough syrup. My tile, your tile, full loaf of bread in the oven, pot of coffee, coil of rope neat on the stairs. What I etched on your skin became mine, became yours again when I let you. A name is just a room to live in; I call you anything. I seed the front yard with vowel sounds, pock-marked consonants. No one yells today on my decision. Some stray sound populates the fenced-in yard. Hummingbirds go after the salvia in the front bed outside the window. We question how hummingbirds live. I imagine large covens of them, fully constructed houses hidden away in tall trees. You say they must live on light, set up shop in the rays of the sun. To be so small and weightless. They don't like when we're in the yard and they want to taste something. Nasturtium and hollyhock line the house, wild rose the back porch. They swoop to and fro, unseen, and sound like tiny semis.

NEON LIGHT OF FALLING STARS

In the sink, the leafy tops of carrots, curve of molded onion, the dog hair and red mud you rinsed off your hands. We're supposed to see stars tonight, the Perseids, but you're tired. I wanted to be gone by morning, but can't shake the headache and refuse to drive blind. The distance between my face and the window, between the hot water in my hands and the fogged glass hums. I turn off the water and the space still hums and the glass stays wet with the heat. In the shed the bulb light snaps off and I watch you cover the yard with your anger, hands down at your sides. They don't really move when you walk, not when you're like this. And then you look up. There was a moment in Vegas when I really believed you knew how neon worked. Gas stranded in a tube, something about numbers. Then you lost everything we had, also about numbers, including the fifty you made from selling my watch. The man in the pawnshop thought we were criminals, like everyone else, working at ruining lives. He held a toothpick in his mouth so long, the sogged wood wouldn't leave his lip when he spit. We won't ever be like him. His smoke-yellow hair. Night-driving, no money to pay the hotel. When the car stalled in the desert we saw stars, they were like this, falling and new.

THE BALANCE OF TERROR

In the blue room it's always five past seven. Your father broke both your arms. *The balance of terror*, he said. You wrote for nineteen weeks with your feet, nothing legible, but you were angry and the words felt right. Scraggly X's over everyone's names. The dung hull of the rudderless ship. And everything moving or everything not. Pale sky with clouds, haze, smoke. Pale sky like a blank sheet of paper. Pale you with that bruise on your arm, sucked in cheeks like air's being pulled from the top of your head. The neighbor came over with a stack of our mail, saying something's not right with that mailman. You had blank black eyes with that circle of blue; he could see right through you. And me standing in the kitchen doorway, saying silently *not this time, not this time*, eyeing the shotgun leaned against the wall. Bird in the fire and he spied this, saying nothing's wrong. *Not this time.* "Jackass looks like papa. Cocksucker beats his dog." Maybe one day soon someone will hit him and that will be the end of it. Half the mail's been opened. Steamed like no one'd notice. What's better, say, a city or a room? You watch the clock and wait for the next dose, so patient, so calm, and so still.

HESITATION CUT

The boy came in and put his head down on the sofa and lifted his feet one two onto the sofa and I wanted to know his name but instead asked if he wanted any water. "What?" he said. "Water," I said. "Would you like some?" And the boy fell asleep without answering, one shoe on the couch's soft pile, one shoe dangling like supernatural enchantment from an ultra white tube sock ringed with red and yellow stripes. I thought I might harm him if I knew his name. What was he doing here? I thought. And was he one of yours? Another I'd not met before? I touched his hair. I knuckled his chin. Was his face, his thin, fine chest captured inside your camera? I wanted to crack his nose or I wanted to kiss him. I wanted to slice his ear with a penknife or I wanted to kiss him. I wanted to wake him, shaking your father's rifle at his cock or I wanted to cover his mouth with my mouth and breathe all the boy from him. In the kitchen I cracked the metal tray, exposing ice to the jar. I ran the brown water clear, I ran the water cold.

TO BREAK OR BURN

You stand alone, stiff limbs in the pasture. Your mother used both onion and glass rod to collect disease. **I will have nothing to do with this**. Glass wiped once upon waking with a fresh white cloth. But will bleach your clothes, burn them in the fire pit. Fresh rag charred. Move the stones into a heart shape. Onion replaced once it lost its smell, three days. "Meaty," you say. You close your fist. Four days in. You're left with nothing. What was the point? You didn't learn anything about morphology or empathy. "A long walk." The wild onion fields were endless. Burn it in the dry creek bed, burn it 'til you're warm. Everything begins in soil. It all begins with fire.

SAINTE-VICTOIRE

"Cezanne left paintings he didn't like in the fields," I
say. The television is the most interesting thing in
the room. Your eyes are glazed and make me think
of heel blisters burst wet. The girl on the screen
misses the beam, a man covers her face with his
hand. "Get me a drink," I say. I don't really want one.
I just want to know that you'll care for me when I get
old. "What about the Sainte-Victoire?" you say. And
the tarn cleaves deeper, and a mountain made out of
blue clay and lavender dashes grows on your chair.

PRODUCE

We're in the grocery store and the boy behind the meat counter is looking at you. Blond boy with plastic gloves of rudimentary cleanness, the kind that doesn't go far. He's got dried blood ringing his elbow and a sadness in his eyes you'll want to know about. We're in the grocery store and the man with red hands smells oranges while he looks at you. He squeezes peaches until they fall apart, fleshy and wet on his pants, pooled on the linoleum, sweet stain of fluorescence. We're in the grocery store, or I've got you on the hood of the car. I've got you in the back seat with your hands tied behind you. You're on your face, whining about the taste of leather again. A man stands behind you in line. He flips through magazines and he catches your eye, black hair tucked behind his ear, his face a memory of childhood. A man walks into the produce aisle, black hair and black boots and black gaze. He picks tomatoes without looking at them. His hands become claws, become hands again, rooted in fruit, shaking with what could be rage. And you turn like you like him, like his staring at you. Lights dim, focus into spotlight bright on both your faces. His smile never ends. He lays you down, or sits you under that lamp. He's a magician, and you're what he's sawing in half. The boy behind the meat counter is clapping his cellophaned hands.

(3)

BAD WALLPAPER, SUBURBAN HOME

Every night it was the same. The meatloaf was burnt or it wasn't or it wasn't meatloaf at all. I imagined the salads other mothers would have, my father's socks balled under the table, my sister fingering a pocket full of Halls drops. The crinkle like sudden fire.

SPOKES PINCH FINGERS

There is magic in bleeding, it starts with a riddle in the skin, a rip. Someday I will have nothing left to lose. If I die in August, if I die in June, if I die some Monday morning, the week spread out, undeserved. If I wear your leather better, will you wash the summer from me? Breath explodes early white from the sides of your head. **The sun swings low**, it swings low, swings low. Your mother's bad back, mother in the chair. It was a Monday then: Mother's swollen ice pack, Father's willing fist. The ending of a school year. There was no scar, there was no you, no press me into flesh, death, no make me into you. We have a map of the back woods. A map of the hill where the dark loam and old growth rise. I'm afraid to leave you though I have the plan; the green all looks the same. Hardwood, pulp, and sapling. Blue-cap bark and burlesque. All those trees with their terrible hands.

PARNASSIA FIMBRIATA

I could **run** faster than my stepfather's fist. "You say one word." And then I said it. *Always leave the door unlatched*. My mother let me in those hours later. Each night, the wrench in my hand making me feel stronger, just the weight of it. I never thought I'd use it. I spent years against that tree trunk, correcting time, correcting vision. Dog collar around my neck, chain dangling, wrapped around my ankle, **press**ed in harder, fussy skin giving up its liquor. Years later I call the **scar** *tattoo*. In the woods that first **run**, I found a **wreck**ed wall. Grey rocks against grey leaves, grey sky. And just that yellow **flash** of birdfoot trefoil underfoot. I picked up a cool, mudded stone, some big **fist** of earth **and fit** it into what was left of that crumbling hedge. And every day, every run, another—through the woods, electric moss and lichen, yarrow, monkshood and bull thistle, and that sound of spotted towhee, a Steller's jay—what a toxic tune. I put the rocks back, day by day, like moving time, or some **stop**ped clock, back to the **beginning**.

WIFE BEATER

There's a tattooed girl at the counter in the bread shop and she's thin and she's tough and she's scarred and **you** start talking about what her life must be like. Tank top, wife beater, fresh bruise on her chin. **You** wonder if she's somebody's wife. And the shirt doesn't come all the way down to her pants, which are low, which are black, which are ripped at the knee. And the shirt is a **little dirty** around the middle like she'd rubbed up against some dirty truck. And I see your eyes turn down and you look at her waist and **you** whisper something about stretch marks. I tell **you you** have no business speculating about the nature of those. Was she fat, you said, but **you** decide it was babies. And how many. You give her seven babies, but she's probably only twenty-three and just looks forty-four. She hasn't had time, I say and you say, she looks like the world, this girl, she looks like the whole damn world has been sitting right in her lap.

BURNSIDE

I had planned to leave earlier. The problem with loving two of you is remembering who to bite. The car idles in the not-garage. Hinges squeak and swagger like one shaken with drink. I am shaken with drink. I will remember who you are. **You like to** talk rough and kiss lightly, **or are** you the other one? **You** like to take the stairs double. Sometimes **you** fall when you refuse the handrail. **There** in the rubble at the frost fence, I find **your** father's ring. He **had a name** for jukeboxes: bubble machines with song, or song machines with bubble. He liked to make noise. **When** I heard that song again I cried. I was **with** the wrong one. Teeth pinching flesh before I remembered. I set my tongue **down** and made it into something else. What day is **it**? What mood? **What is your name again?** The Burnside flows to the arctic, where my heart is. I found your father's ring. Horses with their flank heat, hunting places paved with **pitchblende**. The rooms we built with limestone, or screams, the fervor. The **soft walls** wail, the soft walls cave. Sometimes we write on them, but lines get lost. Or lives. Something is buried in the yard. Notebook or bone, looseleaf or someone's glass eye. Adagio of wormwood, fingers bent through holes, the perfidy, or rotting. The way your stares wander through me. How you find my open door. You were a safe place once, in the **undersound**. You were the wash of water through the white walls of glacier. The bluewhite walls of glacier. Where my heart's muscle still beats stupidly, conserving heat, melting slow the walls around.

NOTES ON FEEDING

I wait a few minutes for the horse to nose my palm. She's uninterested in my handful of grass. She's uninterested in a Tootsie Roll, wrapped or unwrapped that Fancy forces between her teeth. The air is **muted** yellow with the chaff of thrown hay. There's hay in my hair. Hay in the mare's mane. Fancy's **itchy** and she won't calm down. The horse is tied to the fence in front of us. I can tell she **wants to run**. The sun falls behind the barn. It's cold in shadow. The red shed has seen deader girls. I don't know how to reckon this. You with the answers inked all in. You with lipstick smeared. **You on your knees**. Playing at house with boys, with girls. You call me up, sobbing. We refuse to hang up, admit defeat. I can't take Fancy back. This fence becomes a home. One will make amends. One becomes a dial tone.

LIKE MUSIC WE MIGHT DANCE TO

You **scratch** your arm and wait, victim to the scent of a hundred planes. Jet fuel fouls the sky and your head runs under those silver bellies, screams like a lost trapeze searching for a fist. **Like radio static** reaching for a station through tunnel walls. But **you're still** sitting at the windows, waiting, watching the reflection of passengers walking by, and the girl sitting three seats from you who eats bunless hamburger meat with her hands. You'll fly to me, but it won't be today. You're **lost**, looking up knots on the internet because we want something new, something to prove our bravery, bowline, sheet knot, figure eight and studding sail, a timber hitch. We want the burn on my arms irregular, like music we might dance to. I had that dream again. Your face underwater and blurrily beautiful, blonde hair in your eyes. *Forgive me. I am slightly drunk. This is what I want.* I want you there again. Before the lungs fill, before speech descends into vacancy. You swim away, but I catch you on the other side **where the water clouds with red**. You say, "Guns don't kill; bullets do."

MISSING, FOUND

Yesterday they found a boy's **body** between a log and an abandoned G-P dock, near the warming pool or cooling pool, or whatever they call where they stored water for a while that was too wrong for the bay when the factory was going. The rhomboid that threw me every time I looked at maps of this town before we got here. When we got here I wanted to walk around it, but there are fences everywhere, concertina a heavy halo forbidding. When the factory was going, the water steamed. An always lifting fog.

NIGHT SKY SPECTRUM AND FORBIDDEN TRANSITIONS

Today the sky, an unspeakable shield of grey, keeps us staring in, grey too and too unwashed for love. Of what use is the mirror, when between white marks of wet froth the face is as recognizable as a bowl of decomposing fruit? Sharp steps quicken on **wet** pale wood, or the thunder of a bicycle before the slip. A young man eats breakfast at the bayside grill, picking gristle **like** seaweed from teeth the rocks would **like** to knock.

TWO OR TWO HUNDRED

The new neighbor has two hundred dogs. There's something of a pack mentality to people in jeans. Hands wild at the wheel, I **question** everything but the knocking sound that means we will eventually stall. I question everything but the scan function on the radio. It brings me Mozart, then Jay-Z, some Irving Berlin. *Make yourself comfortable before we start. Tie yourself right up to my side.* You say anxiety deserves expectation, you wanted to be free. You say you used to be like this, and when I ask *like how* you say something about blue jays sounding like monkeys, screeching in trees.

We stop for ice cream. You get two scoops of something with nuts. I get soft serve with that hard waxy shell. We stop for a quart of oil, a quart of milk, both of which will end up on the pavement. And you say you're all wool and a yard wide, which is eight feet shorter than the lane where we lay side by side. Our quart of milk souring at our feet, the oil a constant drip.

WALLS, NOT DOORS

I would like that photo of you with your hands tied behind your back. Your face red, skin wet and wanting. I want the rope in the photo around your neck. I want that picture of you. The one the girl stole and made copies of. That papered the neighborhood like some sick snow. I want to say how can you trust someone who shatters glass whenever she gets the chance. I want to say how can you believe in anything, stars aligning, rotating sun, spots that will slay us, quickly or with cancer. You stand, asking forgiveness for her shaved legs, her impeccable hair, her can't-hold-a-conversation charm. **Sometimes we want** *muteness.* But she wasn't mute. *Sometimes we want stares.* Eyes that go nowhere, walls are not doors. Your twin pockets out, knife gone, lines that never meet. Stay in red rooms, meet me. Or in standing water. Stage children who think of the earth, clay caking, red **needle under the skin**. Close your **eyes, heart**. I want to remember you with your legs crossed at the ankle, shins **lifting off the edge** of the bed.

ERIN BROCKOVICH

You keep the valentine up on the fridge: cardinals beak to beak and a red heart behind them. *Be mine.* I say I met you on the treadmill at the Y, dual runners facing the window, turning up the speed to impress, getting shocked repeatedly. The old, old equipment. And how hot our hands were, tuning our hearts into the machines, beat after beat until they added up to something. The *burn zone.* But none of that is true. Personal ads for anonymous sex sometimes breed love. But it was your mountain bike I got, light rust and its various speeds. The sex that day was elsewhere and mediocre, in a dirty apartment I left itching and still hungry. You and I laughed a lot. You held on to the bike for a time and I looked at your hands. We talked about movies and TV. *Arrested Development* and *CSI*, but mostly about Julia Roberts and how maybe she and her brother Eric were really the same person because we'd never seen them on film together. "Maybe he doesn't exist." "Maybe *she* doesn't." *Erin Brockovich* was not the answer to anything. **There is** a **space between us** that day that one could park *two* bicycles in. I'm not even close enough to grab your arm when you say something witty. My hand touches air and returns to my side. "We should ride together sometime," I say. But you've just given me your only bike.

GO AWAY CLOSER

A cow reminds me of my dog and I'm home again, not still weightless in the train car, reading post-it notes you left in a folder. Yellow scatters on the dirty floor like some mad slow snow, it shifts around. **I'm undone by** the distance, by conversations with strangers, talk starts always with where are you headed or where have you been? No one really listens. Their story always better, judged by main characters who want nothing to do with what's outside strict narrative of here to there, life to death, and don't forget the babies. I want to tell them about you, how you hold me down, how I hold you down, **how you make me forget**. I want to tell them what **love** is. A man from Chicago tells me I'll want babies, tells me I'm ripe for babies, stares me down like he could put a baby right in my lap. Red rocks of plateaus like strange hats in the desert, or something unfinished. Something unfinished waits for me there. I want that broken camera. Shutter release and regret, the release stays open all the time. Too much light will end in darkness. The process stopped. The process speeded up again. I want every picture returned where we were unsmiling. Under the mask, **you**r third person, mine. "But **are** you miserable?" *My face just looks like that.* Every night I dream about you. Every touch is persuasion, seduction, is also a pushing away. The go away closer, the let me love you from here.

THE **MAGNETIC** VIRTUES

I tore a ligament trying to gut **you**, wheat flag smut in another neighbor's field; they said **destroy** by fire. I pulled some secret bone and then went on to name it: You or some other costliness, some other form of abstinence. Sodden matches drying in the sun. And then a flash like lightning, but it was just that boy again. You will not want. What failed in all the time between, err of rising years, err of growing danger in a small tin cup, in the back of a two-toned Ford. Failed in all the side streets. When everything was quiet: before the dam had split, before the floods. How every line of pavement led to a radiance we couldn't know, rapid dash between blinds and everything closing, what washes hands of us. What stills blue and locomotive. Locks lost and winter's tossed east amid families. The ways we won't go home. Places we won't let in, circling hearts like fan blades. For when the ribbon shreds and splits.

THE POINT OF HOLDING

Twice today we've gone the same speed and parallel to a plane landing. Small craft squeaks, large white smoke. There is no stopping without damage. From this I have determined flight to be a beautiful thing. Or at least the ingress. Holding speeds are a function of aircraft weight at the point of **hold**ing. I want to make a metaphor about holding you, but it won't **come**. Pen to sweat, skin too close for focus, defies comparison. The longer the contact—hand to brow, hand to hand, hip to crotch, longer, the hot heavy weight of your mouth on my neck, your pull in my hair—the greater the shake of unmooring. Shadow in the weeds, shadow on the water. Estuaries of emotion dragged for spare parts. A **yes here**, then some may**bes**. I turn you with care. Every poem is a love **one**, or else about sex. An engine turns. A gull talks shit to you, dives at cr**ows**. And then we're in your car. On the tarmac, in the loading zone. An engine stops. One of us must leave. There's a door slam, someone mounts the curb, someone climbs the stairs.

THE SKY IS NEVER BLUE

I had another dream about you when you were gone. Blonde head black in shadow, pressed into the neck and forelock of a russet horse. A man stands in the stall's corner reciting those same three lines of Shakespeare I once learned. The *tongues in trees, books in running brooks, sermons in stones, the good.* Perhaps the man is me, waiting inside witness wood, panels two hundred years old, waiting to be noticed, addressed, understood. I see your face in the grey planks, then in shadow on the mare. The brace on the man's leg kicks out from the wall and settles back noisily. And settles back with a scrape like a popped balloon. Your face stays on the horse and you say soft, then loud to drown my broken voice, my not-so subtle pop and drag, *The sky is never blue, but it's always. The sky is never blue,* **but**. *The sky is never blue.* When I ask how this can be true when I can clearly see the sky (blue) through the high window, and when I ask what it *always* is, **you** say, *To complete a sentence takes time.* And the wood isn't wood, the **wo**od is concrete, the straw ground concrete with flecks of blood in an arc **on t**he floor. And hair settled into seams. Fingernails settled into seams. The horse is a hand-me-down, a blanket scratchy and wool. And the man on the wall is a warden, and the brace is a rifle he holds with two hands.

THE LAST THING I WANT TO DO

I did that thing where I wouldn't put **any**thing in my
mouth for **the** longest time. So I wouldn't lose what
was left of you. Even after taste fades, and the feeling.
Even after thirst makes everything dry. I parch, I
desiccate, die; you replace me.

I rebuild the house from memory all the way home.
The fireplace that holds no fire, the broken TV, that
lamp everyone has. Stains on the carpet; stains on
linoleum. Terra cotta tiles in the foyer, miniature
terra cotta animals hunting pale yellow shelves.
Stone walls, orange low sun, and you standing in the
yard, red face flushed and mud on your arms, your
worn-through shoe with its sliver of duct tape
crowning the toe.

The arborist had taken the tops off all the trees in the
front yard. So they wouldn't crowd the wires. But I
kept thinking: decapitation. Where my head is.
Where is my head? The green, another straight line,
another horizon. How to get to you. What I want is
messier than fire. What I want is soot-black in the
keel, a balance wheel back on its heels. Hairspring
and oscillation, a regulating beat.

You said the clothing got lonely, waiting for me.
Shirts separated by sheets on the line. Thread counts
like miles. Dead weight of my bag in the backseat. I
felt imperfect again moving away from you, listening
as another bee troubled the window like some
runner in a suicide squeeze.

LAST MEAL OF GIN

What it took: two days to get used to. The break-off,
lesion to touch, legion. **And** *where were you when?*
And then admitting that dream. What breaches.
What I would have made up, but didn't. From there,
dories everywhere, talk of unicorns, what horns,
whatever, the red birds that did not alight on my
arms: there was no going back. Everything right
now is about you. Standing in the dim kitchen,
knee-deep in me. Standing in the living room, the
lights clicking **off**. *Timers.* I can't see the face for the
face, can't see the place for the what if. We were a
mob of lost parts, a wreckage of history. Weekends
are tiny models of the world, what weeks want to be.
Sometimes what years. Might contain all electric, all
thought. Which way we went. A tug on the hair and
the clock shakes, pulling you forward by bangs,
waking up bruised. Waking with loss everywhere.

HELLO STOCK FOOTAGE

These are your cityscapes, your farm scenes, your hidden entryways, your B&Bs, your almanacs of possible meadowlands and army cars and airplanes and distant herds of indeterminate animals, and other warm feelings in celluloid. Here we are imagining a baby or a lamb or a tarn or inselberg between us where once there were only pillows and your cast off cardigan. And we get to the part where you won't get me anything and even the melted ice is warming and I'm disgusted by how greasy what I thought were my clean hands have made the glass and I need another drink. "This is your house," I say. You just point to the fridge, and the bottles on top. So close together they clink when the compressor cycles on. **And we get to the part** in the movie **where** the boy says something that makes the girl see he's not such a bad deal after all, and really she doesn't want the good-looking one. But really they're all good-looking because this is TV. "I want life to be like this," I say. And you just roll your eyes without asking. I am waiting for you to kiss me, or waiting for you to make that sound that means you want me to lean over and make a play for your lap.

WHAT THE BODY KNOWS

I want to sit in the front yard and rearrange the apples that have fallen since I left. I'm sure I could spell something complicated out. But there's the rot, hands sticky, slugs finding home. Bees ricocheting off wet neck and forehead, crawling on my arms. I get to an A. And then: *what have I done?* Boiled water in a woodsman's hut. Gun movement, shoe white. There was never any gun. The shoes were never white.

Man standing on a bridge, double bascule, counter-weighted overpass, tall against the lamppost. In the umbra, still, light wouldn't get to him. I stopped the car. I started to get out. The sound of an opened door is the sound of air finding weight.

Wet wind through fur of a hundred crouching dogs, who show teeth, who line the yard. You sold the tractor, the house. Shot the horse, got rid of everything. And then got rid of me. The water never slows in the lost and dark below. No matter now the space between, **the body knows** to swim.

NO ONE WAITS IN THE SIDE YARD

No one waits in the side yard for the light to come on. No moths tick against cold panes. The growl is not a snore though it rises from the bedclothes. Though it rises from stained sheets the scent is not of blood but love. No hat decorates the coat rack. No pale shirt has fallen to the floor. No dog's paw has muddied anything, and you can bet all boots were off. No tighter tight and blue-bright through star-and-moon-punched skylight. No water on the floor. No one did the dishes. No calico ginger-steps the egg pan, purring at the instruments. No half-mined pomegranate pinks the countertop. No cake crumbs below the bread knife. There's no one on the porch. Five cut apples there, cored and rotting in a jar. That glass could slip or freeze. There is no mystery here. No charmed life, no wind or time, no backwards kiss goodbye.

(NOTES)

Title THE CODES OF EVENTUAL LOVE is taken from a passage in *Divisadero* by Michael Ondaatje.

Forgive me. I am slightly drunk. This is what I want. (in LIKE MUSIC WE MIGHT DANCE TO) is from Elisabeth Murawski's "Note From a Train."

Make yourself comfortable before we start. Tie yourself right up to my side (in TWO OR TWO HUNDRED) is from Irving Berlin's "Stop, Stop, Stop (Come Over and Love Me Some More)"

The *tongues in trees, books in running brooks, sermons in stones, the good.* (in THE SKY IS NEVER BLUE) is from Shakespeare's *As You Like It.*

NO ONE WAITS IN THE SIDE YARD is after Rachel Loden's "Glasburyon."

ACKNOWLEDGMENTS

Thanks to Carol Guess, Andrea Danowski, & Piper Daniels, for continued inspiration and multiple reads.

Thanks to John Marshall & Christine Deavel of Open Books, for always putting the right book into my hands. I would not be the writer I am today without your steady guidance.

Thanks to Diane Goettel & Amy Freels, for your care in bringing this book into the world. And to Oliver de la Paz, Debra DiBlasi, & TC Tolbert, for your kindnesses and first reads.

Thanks to Justin Duffus, whose painting appears on the cover.

Thanks to Richard Siken, for your writing.

Thanks to Linda Bierds, Heather McHugh, & Andrew Feld, for vital guidance on the reworking of some of these pieces. Feld, I know there are still a few lines in here you heartily disagree with.

Thanks to my UW cohort(s), Jessica Rae Bergamino, Kate Lebo, Luke Laubhan, Rich Smith, Jay Yencich, Thomas Grout, Emily Sketch Haines, Katie Howes, & Calvin Pierce. JRB & Lebo, you transcend.

Thanks to my colleagues at WWU, for your friendship and conversation on all things art and teaching.

Thanks to my family, Matthew Phillips, Carolynn Thanos, Jean Bos, Louise Bos, Mike Dressel, & Sheri Rysdam, for your love and support and for forgiving if you ever see yourselves weirdly in anything I write. And to Jeff Colen, wherever you are.

This book is haunted affectionately, I hope. Malinda Pierce, Diana Jones, David Bowie, C.D. Wright, rest easy spirits. The world has not been the same in your absence.

And thanks to the editors of the following publications in which these pieces first appeared, sometimes in slightly different versions:

Anti-: "The Magnetic Virtues" and "Two or Two Hundred"

Barn Owl Review: "Burnside" and "Wife Beater"

Burnside Review: "Neon Light of Falling Stars" and "Weightless"

City Arts Magazine: "Inside the Lost Museum"

Columbia Poetry Review: "Bad Wallpaper, Suburban Home"

Connotation Press: "A Drowning, 1984," "Expanded Cinema" and "Sainte-Victoire"

Dos Passos Review: "Ravine"

deComp: "Missing, Found"

Everyday Genius: "Notes on Feeding"

The Far Field: "Episodic Tremor and Slip," "The Perfect Kind of Happy," "Orders of Magnitude," and "On Snow" (as "Episodic Tremor and Slip")

Filter Literary Journal: "Cartography" and "Red Angles of a Curious Past"

Flicker and Spark Anthology: "Erin Brockovich"

Hoarse: "Memory of Light" and "To Break or Burn"

Juked: "The Codes of Eventual Love"

Metazen: "Breadfruit," "Low Clouds" and "Waiting for the Damage"

Midwestern Gothic: "Diagram of a Camera"

The Monarch Review: "Go Away Closer" and "No Smoking, No Open Flames"

out of nothing: "What the Body Knows," "The Public Showers," "Like Music We Might Dance To," "The Sky is Never Blue," "Walls, Not Doors," and "No One Waits in the Side Yard" (as "This is Meant to Bring You Back")

PANK: "Hesitation Cut," "Parnassia Fimbriata," "Shot-Silk Effect, No. 1," "Shot-Silk Effect, No. 2," "Shot-Silk Effect, No. 3," and "Shot-Silk Effect, No. 4"

Portland Review: "The Last Thing I Want to Do"

Spillway: "Spokes Pinch Fingers" and "We Are Only Animals Furred and Undone"

Sou'wester: "Throatlatch and Longeing"

Spork Press: "Your Mother Know You Ride Like That," "Buckshot and Diesel," "Someone With Keys," "The Balance of Terror," and "Produce" (all 5 poems reprinted in 2015's &NOW Awards 3)

Sweet: "Duplication" (as "Dark Stones")

Thumbnail Magazine: "Contamination Anxiety, No. 1," "Contamination Anxiety, No. 2," and "Contamination Anxiety, No. 3" (as "Uptown Girl")

Women's Quarterly: "Hello Stock Footage"

Elizabeth J. Colen was born in Wichita, KS and has lived in three corners of the U.S. She is the author of poetry collections *Money for Sunsets* (Lambda Literary Award finalist in 2011) and *Waiting Up for the End of the World: Conspiracies*, flash fiction collection *Dear Mother Monster Dear Daughter Mistake*, long poem / lyric essay hybrid *The Green Condition*, and fiction collaboration *Your Sick* (co-written with Carol Guess and Kelly Magee). She teaches at Western Washington University.